I love bugs!

For Conrad and Imogen
with all the love in the world
Emma xx

Text and illustrations copyright © Emma Dodd 2010
First published in 2010 by Orchard Books
338 Euston Road, London NW1 3BH
Orchard Books is a division of Hachette Children's Books,
an Hachette UK company.
www.hachette.co.uk
The right of Emma Dodd to be identified as the author and
illustrator of the work has
been asserted by her in accordance with
the Copyright, Designs and Patents Act 1988.
First published in the United States of America
by Holiday House, Inc. in 2010
All Rights Reserved
HOLIDAY HOUSE is registered in the U.S. Patent
and Trademark office.
Printed and Bound in July 2010 in Shenzhen, China,
at Shenzhen Wing King Tong Paper Products Co., Ltd.
www.holidayhouse.com
3 5 7 9 10 8 6 4
Library of Congress Cataloging-in-Publication Data
Dodd, Emma, 1969-
I love bugs / by Emma Dodd. — 1st American ed.
p. cm.
Summary: Easy-to-read text celebrates the many kinds
of bugs that can be found in a backyard.
ISBN 978-0-8234-2280-7 (hardcover)
ISBN 978-0-8234-2345-3 (paperback)
[1. Insects—Fiction. 2. Spiders—Fiction.] I. Title.
PZ7.D6626Ial 2010
[E] — dc22
2009032814

I love bugs!

Emma Dodd

Holiday House / New York

I love all bugs...

big

and

small bugs.

I love springy

jumpy leapy
bugs

and

slimy
crawly
creepy
bugs.

I love hard spiky spiny bugs and pretty spotty shiny bugs.

I love fuzzy sunny honey bugs

and **furry** whirry funny bugs.

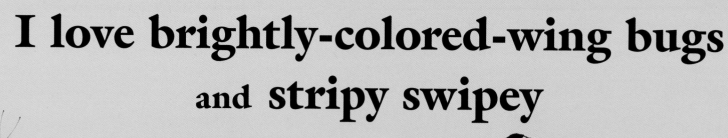

I love brightly-colored-wing bugs
and **stripy swipey**

sting bugs.

I love whiny-buzzy-

sound bugs

and glide-across-the-ground bugs.

I love
flouncy

frilly

flutter
bugs

and silly clitter-clutter
bugs.

I love fly-around-the-light bugs and curl-up-tight bugs.

Yes, I love all bugs! Hop

nd **fly** and **crawl bugs.**

But the best bugs are hairy bugs. Eight-legged scary bugs.

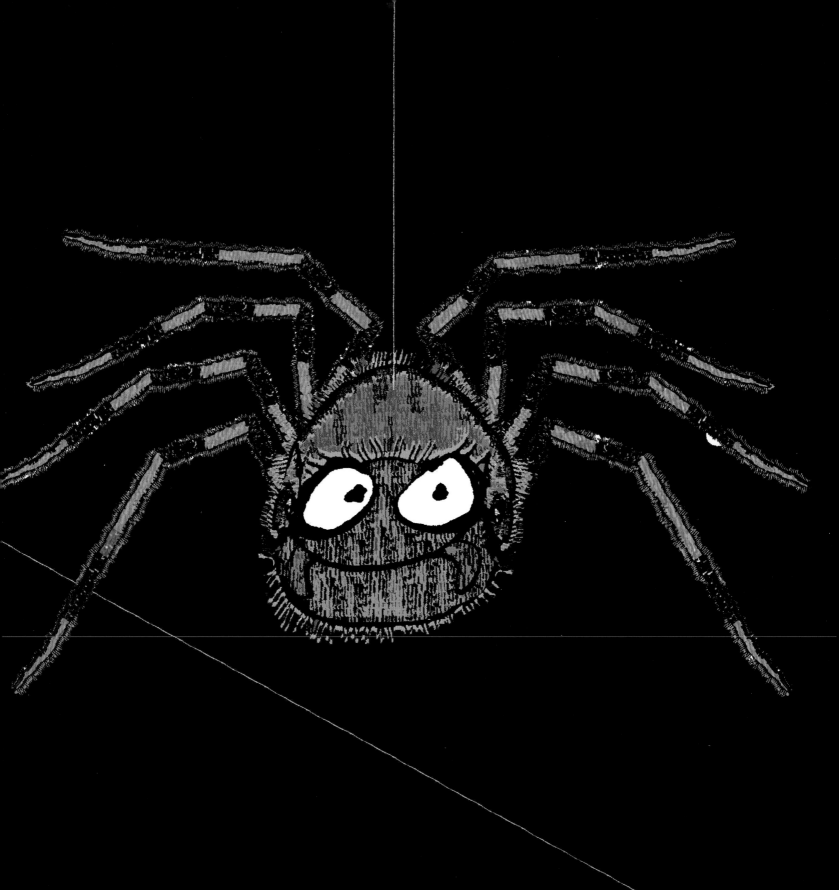

The hang-from-the-ceiling bugs . . .

and send-me-squealing bugs!